Dark Diary

DEAD RINGER

by

ANTHONY MASTERS

To Mary Hamley
who shared the vision

ORCHARD BOOKS
96 Leonard Street, London EC2A 4XD
Orchard Books Australia
14 Mars Road, Lane Cove, NSW 2066
First published in Great Britain in 2000
Paperback original
Text © Anthony Masters, 2000
The right of Anthony Masters to be identified as the
author of this work has been asserted by him
in accordance with the Copyright,
Designs and Patents Act, 1988.
A CIP catalogue record for this book is
available from the British Library.
ISBN 1 86039 943 6
1 3 5 7 9 10 8 6 4 2
Printed in Great Britain

Wednesday, 14th

It's 11.30pm and I should have been asleep hours ago, but there are so many thoughts racing through my head I just can't relax. I need to think, to try and make sense of it all. I never thought I'd bother with this diary, but after today, I want to jot down everything that happens. I hope it'll help to jog my memory, to identify the voice on the phone. The voice sounds so familiar, but I still can't place it. I don't know why, but I feel really scared. Perhaps I'm trying to stop myself remembering — But why would I want to do that?

The phone was driving them all mad. For the past two hours it had rung constantly, but whenever Steve or his parents picked up the receiver there was never anyone there.

The phone company told them they had a serious computer fault at the exchange, and were doing their best to make repairs.

Mr Parker had tried to assert his authority by insisting his family didn't answer the phone, but Steve's mother had kept on about Gran – supposing she was ill and needed to get in touch.

In the end, Mr Parker had taken to wearing ear plugs, but Steve was sure he could still hear the ringing.

2

It's now midnight, but I still can't sleep. The phone's started up again and it's really getting to me. Even with my head under the duvet I can still hear it ringing. The extension's on the landing just outside my bedroom, but it might as well be in here with me. I've got a history test at school tomorrow, but I'll be so tired I'm bound to blow it. Why don't Mum or Dad answer it? It's ringing and ringing and ringing. It's no good, I can't stand it any longer. I'll have to answer it myself...

Steve threw off the duvet and got out of bed, tripping over his skateboard.

When he opened the door the phone was blasting away so loudly that his ears hurt. Why hadn't his parents woken up.

He grabbed the receiver and listened, but there was nothing but static.

5

Then very faintly he heard the voice. 'Are you there?'

'Who is this?' he yelled. 'Who are you?'

But whoever was on the other end of the line didn't reply. It certainly wasn't Gran, for he would know her voice anywhere. Steve listened hard, but the voice was distorted now, almost completely drowned out by the static.

Then, suddenly, for a second, it was more distinct. 'Is that you, Stevie?'

Steve felt incredibly afraid, and his hand was shaking so much he almost dropped the receiver.

Then the static got even louder and he forced himself to replace the receiver and go back to bed. But his mind was racing.

A few minutes later the phone started to ring again.

Steve was so terrified he couldn't move. Why didn't his parents pick it up?

But they didn't seem to hear it, and the phone kept on ringing.

Then, just as Steve could bear it no longer, his father's heavy footsteps thudded along the landing. A low buzzing began and continued for some time until the line went dead. When Steve heard Dad stomping off back to bed, he knew what he'd done. He'd taken the phone off the hook, Gran or no Gran.

Good for him, Steve thought. He listened intently, but couldn't hear a thing.

Steve had been tossing and turning for a long time and was just dozing off when he suddenly thought he knew who the voice on the phone might be.

But of course it wasn't possible – not possible at all. Steve felt sick with fright but kept saying to himself that he'd made an incredibly stupid mistake. He had thought the voice had said, 'Is that you, Stevie?' and no one except Mum called him Stevie any longer. It was too babyish. Except for one person. Someone he had known for a very long time. Someone who had been to playgroup, to primary school and then to Stanbrook High School with him. Someone called Ed.

But Ed *couldn't* be the caller, for Ed had drowned last week.

Dad was grumbling over breakfast, repeating himself, saying he was going to make a formal complaint so many times that Mum eventually shouted at him in exasperation.

'Why don't you write to them and get it over with?'

'I will.'

'Go on then.'

'I'll have my breakfast first.'

'I bet you will.' Mum looked as exhausted as Steve and his father. The constant ringing of the telephone had knocked them all out.

Steve could see that Dad was in a mega rage, crunching burnt toast and turning the pages of the newspaper so fiercely that one of them tore in two.

'I'm not losing my beauty sleep just because the telephone's up the spout. Computers! If I had my way —'

Steve switched off as his father bit into the blackest part of the toast, showering crumbs over the table, and only dimly heard his parents continuing to squabble.

The sunlight was stealing across the windows and the milk float was rattling by outside. The postman was walking up the path, whistling tunelessly, the next-door neighbours' dog was barking and Mr Harris was revving up his car like he did every morning, but Dad was too preoccupied to complain. Life was normal, routine, dull, and in circumstances like these you didn't receive telephone calls from the dead.

Steve's best friend Ed had drowned in the River Don last week. His body had been discovered face-down, slowly drifting with the current. Ed had told his parents he was going to rent a video in town, but he had never returned home, and when his mother and father began to search they didn't take long to find him – the path by the river was the short cut everyone took to get to the shops. The inquest had established that there was no sign of foul play, and in the absence of witnesses had delivered a verdict of death by misadventure. Ed had always been a daredevil and everyone was sure he had been messing about on the water's edge and had somehow fallen in. And yet how could Ed have drowned in such calm water? It was all a horrible mystery.

Steve had been in a state of shock ever since. He couldn't believe he would never see Ed again. Ed had been in his life for ever, and that, Steve told himself, was why he thought he had heard his voice shouting through the static. But of course he must have been mistaken.

Suddenly, the telephone began to ring and the whole family started, looking at each other accusingly. Steve wondered which of his parents had replaced the receiver last night. Mum probably. She couldn't bear untidiness and a telephone receiver dangling off the hook definitely fell into that category.

'Leave it!' shouted Dad.

'What about Gran?'

'I said – leave it!'

But Mum was already hurrying across the room and reaching for the receiver. Steve and his father listened, despite the fact they were both pretending not to.

'Hello, Mary. Do you want to speak to your son?' Mum smiled triumphantly as Dad lumbered across the room to take Gran's call.

Steve tried to reason with himself as he walked to school, the summer morning bright and brisk around him. The parade of shops, the bus stop, the zebra crossing, the telephone box, the shabby school buildings – he'd seen them so many times before and they never changed. Why should they? How could anything ever happen here that wasn't grey and boring? So how could he possibly receive a phone call from Ed? Ed was dead.

Steve found himself staring at the telephone box with a strange expectation, until the urgent ringing shrilled out and his heart began to thump.

Why didn't he just walk on? He'd be late for school if he didn't. So why *didn't* he? Why was he rooted to the spot, as if a giant hand had grabbed him, gripping him tight?

There were quite a few people around, going to work and school, while the traffic moved slowly past, bumper to bumper, with the occasional irritable hoot.

Still no one answered the phone. But why should they? It wasn't for them and it wasn't for him either. Was it? Steve felt sick and cold and indecisive.

Then, as if he was being dragged by an irresistible force, Steve ran towards the box, opened the door, grabbed the receiver and listened to the static, which seemed even more dense than before, like some kind of electronic blanket.

The small space was smelly and claustrophobic, and because of the traffic noise outside Steve wasn't sure whether he could hear a voice or not. The sweat was forming beads on his forehead and there was a nasty taste in his dry mouth. *Was* someone shouting his name, desperately trying to communicate?

Trembling, Steve put down the receiver, picked it up again and listened as the familiar buzzing invited the caller to dial.

He pushed open the door of the telephone box, letting in a gentle breeze. Why was he getting so worked up? It had to be the shock of Ed's death. Steve had lost his best friend and he still couldn't believe he was dead. The finality of it was terrible.

He had attended Ed's funeral, seen his coffin lowered into the grave, but he couldn't cry or show any emotion. All he felt was a vast hollow feeling inside.

Steve remained in the phone box for a moment, trying to picture Ed in his mind. But he couldn't. When he had first heard that he was dead he had been incredulous for he could still see Ed. But now he could hardly remember what he looked like and that made him feel worse than ever.

They'd been friends for so long, and had

grown up accepting everything about each other without the slightest hint of criticism although they were so different. Chalk and cheese, as Mum had said so many annoying times. But now she didn't mention Ed at all, and he wondered if she had blanked him out of her mind, put Ed behind her, as if he had never existed.

Steve checked the street outside, but remained in the phone box. He knew he was making himself late, but his mind was full of thoughts of Ed, and he needed time to sift them through.

They had been so different. Steve loved football; Ed hated sport. Steve couldn't concentrate in class; Ed always did well at school. Steve was tall for his age with a mop of dark, crinkly hair like his dad; Ed was small and skinny with blond hair like his mother. Steve's father was a builder, his mother a cleaner and they lived on an estate. Ed lived in a big detached house near the station from which his parents commuted each day. So what did they have in common? Why had they stuck together all these years?

Steve knew the answer. Like him, Ed hated routine, and refused to let it dominate his life.

He was a daredevil and Steve was soon sharing his adventures, climbing to the top of the highest tree, running through an old abandoned railway tunnel with its bats and cobwebs, jumping rocks at Farthing Heights, spending a night in old Mrs Robinson's empty house after she had died, camping out in Slade Wood during a thunder storm. Ed had made life worth living, for like a magician he always made the ordinary extraordinary.

Steve felt tears pricking the back of his eyes and he blinked them away. He hadn't allowed himself to think like this before, not even when his father had taken him outside into the summer garden and told him the dreadful news. He had felt as if a piece of his soul had been sliced away.

Life without Ed was no life at all.

'Coming out?' Ed had always asked when he turned up on Steve's doorstep.

'You bet I am.'

Of course they had both got hurt on several occasions, with more than their fair share of cuts and bruises, including a broken leg for Steve and a fractured collarbone for Ed.

Both sets of parents complained, but they had

never been able to split them up. Sometimes, in his worst moments, Steve wondered whether his mother was relieved that Ed was dead.

Of course their friendship had suffered when big burly Gary arrived from at their school and somehow wormed his way into Ed's life. Unfortunately Gary's idea of adventure was trespassing, jumping trains and bunking off school. Steve hadn't wanted anything to do with him ever since they had all three explored an abandoned brickworks and Gary had started breaking the place up. Ed had only seemed amused and Steve had walked out on them both.

After a while, Ed divided his friendship between the two of them, and although Steve was angry and hurt, he at least had other friends. But he never lost sight of the fact that he considered Gary bad news. Very bad news.

Steve jumped as the phone began to ring again, gazing down at the receiver uneasily. Why had he stayed in the box so long? It was as if he had been waiting for the phone to ring again.

Steve summoned up a burst of energy and managed to half open the door. Then he saw

Gary crossing the road towards him and he made a grab for the phone. But before he could pick up the receiver the ringing had stopped, and Steve felt a strange pang of disappointment.

3

Thursday, 15th

Another fun-packed day at school to
look forward to. At least I won't
have to listen to the phone ringing.
I've decided not to take any more
notice of the calls. Like Dad,
they're really getting to me. Unlike
Dad, I'm going to forget about
them.

I'm so tired I'm already looking
forward to going to bed!

Steve hadn't seen Gary since Ed had drowned
and he didn't ever want to see him again.
Desperately, he picked up the telephone and
pretended to dial, hoping Gary would go away.
But instead he tapped on the glass, and as Steve
mouthed words into the receiver, he felt Gary's,
eyes boring into him.

Then, to Steve's immense relief, Gary
appeared to lose interest, walking away, hands in

17

pockets, swaggering slightly. As Steve watched him go, his mouth continued to open and close though no sound came out.

Steve had never understood why Ed had continued to go around with Gary. What could he have seen in him? Gary was a bully and most people kept out of his way. Had Ed genuinely enjoyed his dodgy adventures? Or was he being bullied into them? He had often wondered about this. Now he wondered even more.

Once Steve had tried to confront Ed when they had been making a tree house in the woods, a shaky platform in the highest branches of an old, weathered oak.

'You're going around with that Gary then,' Steve had begun.

'Yeah.'

'What do you do?'

'Hang around.'

'He's a nasty bit of work.'

'Is he?'

'You like hanging around with a nasty bit of work?'

'It's OK.'

Steve knew he had pushed his warning as far as he could.

Because he was thinking so hard, Steve had forgotten to keep up his pretence of talking on the phone and was now standing in the box, staring ahead, seeing his own worried face in the fly-blown mirror.

Suddenly, he felt a hostile presence again, and saw Gary had returned to leer at him through the smudgy glass. Feeling even more of an idiot, Steve mouthed a 'goodbye', replaced the receiver and opened the door.

'What you doing in there then?'

'Having a shower. Water wasn't hot enough though.'

'Making a call?'

'So that's what these funny-looking boxes are for.'

'Phone's been playing tricks,' said Gary. 'All over town.'

'Magic tricks?'

There was a long silence. Then Gary said awkwardly, 'Bad about Ed.'

'Yeah.'

'Go to his funeral?'

'Yeah.'

'I didn't fancy it.' They stood in silence for a

few moments. Then Gary flung his bag over his shoulder and hurried away. Steve knew he wouldn't come back. But why had he so badly wanted to make contact? Was he feeling guilty about something? Or was he enjoying being threatening?

The classroom was hot. Steve had a splitting headache and was wondering if there was going to be yet another storm in a whole week of them.

He'd managed to complete most of the questions in the history test and didn't think he'd done too badly, so feeling quietly confident, he let his mind return to Ed. He needed to explain to himself why he had been stupid enough to imagine Ed's voice on the phone. Steve remembered what his mother had told him about the sudden death of her sister a few years ago. 'She'd only phoned me the day before. And every time that phone rang, for week after week, I thought it was going to be Sarah on the line.'

There it was – a perfectly reasonable explanation.

After all, Ed had been constantly on his mind. Steve missed him badly and the fact that his death had been followed by a fault on the computer at the exchange was just an unlucky coincidence. The phone kept ringing and the hurt about Ed wouldn't go away.

Steve had always thought he had known Ed inside out, but when Gary had pushed his way in he had wondered if he'd ever really known his best friend. But now Steve was sure that Ed couldn't possibly have liked Gary. Suddenly he began to wonder if Gary had had some kind of hold over Ed.

Steve checked over his test answers, made a couple of alterations and then sat back, waiting for the bell to ring. After a while, he jerked upright, realising he had almost fallen asleep. Gazing intently at the sheet of questions again, Steve tried to avoid the probing gaze of the invigilator, Mr Wentworth, who he was sure had noticed him nodding off.

When the bell eventually went, he hurried out of the hall with Terry, one of his football friends, who was refreshingly normal and full of common sense. So much so that in the past Steve had found Terry rather boring, totally without the adventurous spirit which had made Ed so interesting. But at least Steve always knew where he was with Terry, and right now he welcomed his ordinary, everyday common sense approach.

'Bit tricky.' Terry always said that after tests and exams, particularly if he knew he had done badly. 'Didn't you think so?'

'Sort of.'

'What's that meant to mean then?'

'What it says. You got stuck?'

'The questions weren't easy.' Terry paused. 'You know that one about Charles I?'

'Yeah?'

'Didn't he have a girlfriend who sold oranges?'

'No. That was the other Charles. Charles I was beheaded after the Civil War.'

'Oh.' Terry sounded deflated.

'You got it wrong?'

Steve was surprised for he was the one who usually found the questions difficult. He could never really concentrate hard enough in class, always thinking about something else, like tactics for next Saturday's league match, or an adventure with Ed. Then he realised once again that there wouldn't *be* any more adventures with Ed and he felt cold and empty inside.

'What about Saturday then?' asked Steve, changing the subject.

'What about it?'

'Think we'll win?'

'Only if –' Terry was more confident now as he began to talk tactics, but Steve had already switched off.

Terry was still droning on about football as they passed the school office. But the only thing Steve heard was the sound of the telephone ringing. For a moment Steve froze. But then he got a grip on himself and began to walk on slowly. Why was he reacting so stupidly to the sound of something as ordinary as a phone?

'What's up?'

'Nothing.'

The telephone had stopped ringing.

'You're in a funny mood,' said Terry.

'What do you mean?'

'You scared of something? You look as if –'

Steve froze again as the voice of Mrs Milford, the school secretary, pierced his eardrums like a needle.

'Steven Parker!'

'Milford got it in for you? What's been happening? You cheeked her or something?'

'Shut up!'

Mrs Milford had opened the door of her office and was standing disapprovingly on the threshold. She was tall, thin and angular, with shoulders like a coat hanger and a narrow, unsmiling face.

Steve stared at her apprehensively. 'Yes, miss?' he asked reluctantly.

'There's a call for you.'

'For me?' He felt sick and his mouth was so dry he could hardly speak.

'Pupils are not permitted calls at school,' Mrs Milford grated. 'It's bad enough with the telephones ringing all the time because of this fault at the exchange. Your caller says it's important, but I sincerely hope there's no prank involved.'

'Who is it?' asked Terry.

'Mind your own business, Wooding.'

'Sorry, miss.'

'I couldn't make out the identity of the caller because there's static on the line, but you'd better come into the office, just in case.' Mrs Milford softened slightly. 'We're all sorry about poor Ed. It was such a tragic death and you were his best friend, weren't you?'

Steve nodded.

'Anyway, be as quick as you can on this call.'

'Could you make out *anything* they said?'

'Something about Stevie. "I want to speak to Stevie Parker. It's very urgent."'

Once again Steve felt as if he couldn't move, as if nothing could ever induce him to put one foot in front of the other.

Meanwhile, Terry was gazing at him with mounting curiosity. 'What's going on?' he said. 'Anything I can do?' He was genuinely concerned.

'The only thing I want *you* to do is to clear off,' snapped Mrs Milford.

But Terry stayed where he was.

With an immense effort of will, Steve pushed himself into action, almost running towards the school office. 'Which phone?'

'The one on the desk.'

Terry tried to edge into the office as well, but Mrs Milford was too quick for him, slamming the door in his face.

Steve picked up the phone, only to hear the now familiar sound of buzzing static. He listened intently, but the noise only grew louder. Then a voice came through distantly.

'Stevie —'

'Who is it?'

'Stevie —'

'I'm here. Who is it?' Steve's voice was just above a whisper, conscious not only of Mrs Milford but now Gary, too, gazing through the half-open glass hatch. Where had he come from so suddenly? Terry was also there and his audience was growing.

'Who is it?' Steve gasped, still trying to keep his voice down.

Then he heard his name again, slightly clearer, as if a tide had drawn away from a pebble shore.

'Stevie?'

'Yes?'

The static returned, raging in his ears, almost as if the noise was deliberately trying to cover up something he shouldn't be hearing. Then dimly, very dimly, Steve was conscious of the voice very faintly getting through again.

'I got drowned, didn't I?'

The statement was weird, impossible, and Steve wondered if he had heard it right.

The static closed in again, so loud now that Steve's ears hurt. Then the line went dead.

'Have you finished?' asked Mrs Milford.

'Drowned,' Steve said in a monotone. 'He said "drowned".'

'*What?*' exclaimed Gary, still lingering by the glass hatch.

Steve's head buzzed like the static and their eyes locked.

'What is it? Is something wrong?' Mrs Milford obviously hadn't heard what he had said, but she sounded worried.

'I don't know. I couldn't hear.'

'This telephone business,' she said helplessly. 'The voice was so faint. Did it sound like anyone you know?'

Steve began to sway slightly as blood pounded in his temples and the office grew slightly hazy.

Mrs Milford put a hand on his shoulder. 'Do you want to sit down?' she asked, her voice surprisingly gentle.

Steve slumped down into the nearest chair. He was sure that Gary had heard what he had said for he was staring back at him, pale and transfixed. Mrs Milford stood beside Steve, a hand comfortingly on his shoulder. Outside, Terry was watching Gary who was watching Steve.

Conscious of the intrusion, Mrs Milford wheeled round on the uninvited audience. 'What do *you* want?' she demanded.

'Nothing, miss,' said Gary bleakly.

'Then go away.'

Terry tried to intervene. 'Anything I can –'

'You go away too!' shouted Mrs Milford.

They both went and Steve felt a wave of relief. His hands were damp with sweat but he felt a little less muzzy now as he gazed at the telephone and shivered. It crouched there like a lethal weapon. Why had Gary turned up again? He had looked so angry.

'Would you like to go to the sick room?' Mrs Milford asked.

'I'm feeling better, thanks.'

'You don't look it.'

'These phones,' Steve muttered.

She sighed. 'They're an awful nuisance. But I suppose someone will sort out the problem soon. Shall I ring your mother?' They were almost companionable in the face of the crisis at the telephone exchange.

'I'd rather stay at school.'

'You're sweating. You look as if you've had a shock –'

The telephone began to ring again and they both jumped.

Mrs Milford picked up the receiver, nodded a couple of times and then looked down at Steve. 'I'm so sorry,' she said.

He felt a new kind of rising anxiety. Now what was happening?

'Did you try to ring before?' She was being very sympathetic. 'Yes, this exchange business is frustrating, isn't it? Anyway, Steven is still here.' She handed over the receiver. 'It's your mother. Don't try and stand up. Just keep sitting down.'

'Mum?'

'Not to worry, dear –'

'Worry about what?'

'Your gran's had a bit of a stroke.' His mother's voice was tight and bright, trying to mask her anxiety and failing.

'Stroke –' Steve could hardly understand what she was saying. His life seemed to be running completely out of control on every level.

'I'm phoning from the hospital. The line's been –'

'Is she going to be all right?' he interrupted.

'I'm sure she is.' But the unnatural brightness

in his mother's voice made Steve increasingly uneasy.

'Can I see Gran?'

'Tonight. When she's a bit more comfy. Don't worry, Stevie. She's going to be all right.' Mum sounded as if she was almost pleading with him to agree.

'Did you try to phone before?'

'Lots of times. These lines –'

'Did you get through to me?' Steve asked impatiently.

'I thought I heard your voice.'

'What did you say?'

'What I've just said about Gran. Are you all right?'

'Sort of.'

'You mustn't worry. I told you –'

'She's going to be all right,' repeated Steve dully.

'After tea we'll both go and see her.'

'OK.'

His mother tried to reassure him again, but when she rang off Steve felt angry with her for a reason he didn't understand. Maybe it was because she had treated him like a child.

'It's my gran,' he told Mrs Milford, his voice

wobbling. 'She's not well. She's had…a bit of a stroke.'

'Your mother told me. I'm so sorry, but I'm sure –'

'There's nothing to worry about,' he said flatly. 'The first call. Was that from my mother too?'

'Must have been.' Mrs Milford was brisk now, but still kind and comforting. 'You just didn't recognise her voice with all that crackling. I'm going to get on to the telephone company again. We can't put up with this any longer –' Her voice tailed away. 'Look…are you sure you don't want to go and have a lie down in the sick room? You've really been in the wars. What with Ed, and now your gran. I can speak to the nurse and –'

'No thanks, miss. I'll go to class.'

'Shall I write you a note?'

'I can explain.'

'Very well.' Mrs Milford's voice was gentle. 'I'm so sorry.'

4

Terry wrote Steve a note during French which he passed down the line of desks. It read: ARE YOU OK? WHAT WAS GOING ON? YOUR FRIEND, TEL.

Steve's eyes filled with tears and he ducked down so that he could blink them away without anyone seeing. Terry was a good mate, but he didn't want him. Not now. He only wanted Ed. Even so, Steve wrote back: MY GRAN'S HAD A STROKE. He paused, not knowing how to end. Then he wrote: YOUR FRIEND, STEVE.

At the end of the lesson, feeling exhausted and guilty, he managed to avoid Terry in the crush in the corridor. All he could think about was his gran who he loved deeply. Suppose she died?

At lunch, Steve avoided Terry again, and headed out across the playing field. His anxiety about his grandmother and the voice on the phone had merged together and he needed time to think.

Your gran's had a bit of a stroke. I got drowned,

didn't I? I got drowned, didn't I? Your gran's had a bit of a –

Suddenly Steve realised he had arrived at Puffers' Paradise, more officially known as the football changing rooms where the smokers usually gathered with their roll-ups. Fortunately, there was no one around as he gazed down at the dog-ends and sweet papers and empty cans with unusual satisfaction. This was the real world – untidy, scruffy normality where nothing could happen that was out of the ordinary. He glanced back at the playground where boys kicked a ball around, girls talked in groups and younger kids ran about aimlessly.

The caretaker was creosoting a shed, a dinner lady rode her bike majestically across the grass from the kitchens, her legs straining at the pedals and a couple of teachers strode purposefully towards the science lab, laughing and talking. But Steve's fears didn't subside.

Suddenly he heard footsteps behind him and spun round to find himself face to face with an aggressive-looking Gary.

'What have you been up to?'

'What do you mean?' Steve played for time.

'You were on the phone in Milford's office.'

'I was talking to my mum. But I couldn't hear properly. There's a fault at the exchange.' The phrase was becoming over-used, like a teacher's stale warning. 'Walk, don't run down the corridors.' *There's a fault at the exchange.* 'If you don't work harder, I'm putting you into detention.' *There's a fault at the exchange.*

There was a long silence and Steve had the notion he and Gary were fighting a duel and their swords had locked together.

'What kind of fault?' asked Gary suspiciously.

'You should know. It's all over town.'

'You shouted out something when you were on the phone.' Gary's grey eyes were fixed on Steve, cool and calculating.

'Did I? I can't remember –'

'Something about someone drowning.'

'If you know what I said, why ask?' Steve reckoned he could risk a little hostility of his own.

'What did you mean?'

Steve hesitated. He wanted to wind Gary up and keep him guessing. It was a sudden instinct and it took him by surprise. Where had the idea come from? 'My mum was telling me not to walk back by the river,' he said deliberately.

'Why?'

'That's where Ed drowned. She's funny that way.'

'What do you mean?' Gary's hostility had gone, to be replaced by alarm.

Why am I doing this, wondered Steve with increasing bewilderment. Strangely, he no longer felt in charge of what he was saying.

'She's worried I might fall in too.'

There was an uneasy silence.

'Those things don't happen twice,' said Gary.

'No,' said Steve, sounding unconvinced.

'So why worry?'

The bell went, but neither of them moved. Normality had disappeared again and Steve felt he was in a place he didn't recognise and couldn't understand. Even the graffiti-ridden concrete of the changing rooms seemed to shimmer in the pale sunlight like an alien city.

Gary was the first to turn away, breaking into a lumbering run, but as he neared the science lab a telephone began to ring.

He slowed down and gazed back at Steve uneasily.

Then the ringing stopped.

5

It's 3.30pm, and I'm sitting in the classroom scribbling this. Today has been totally weird, and I don't think it's over yet. First of all there was the phone call at school - that really freaked me out. Of course I didn't hear what I thought I heard, 'I got drowned, didn't I?'

I've written it down so I can see how stupid it looks. It's all in my imagination. It has to be. But it's un-nerving me all the same - the voice really sounded like Ed. As if that's not enough, I've got Gary to deal with as well. He's acting really strangely. It feels as if he's following me, trying to find out something. But what? I've got to find out.

Steve walked home along the river bank, worrying about his gran. Suppose she'd got worse? Suppose she'd died? All Mum's reassurances seemed false and patronising, for Steve only had one grandmother left and he loved her dearly. Sometimes he found it easier to talk to her than his parents. If only he could see her now. She'd soon straighten out this mess for him.

Heavy rain from the recent thunderstorms had swollen the river, and it raced along beside Steve with driftwood and a green plastic garden chair floating on the surface. He had never seen the Don look so malevolent, so threatening.

But when Ed had drowned, the river had been calm. So how could the tragedy have occurred? Steve shuddered as he began to run along the bank.

Once again he had managed to avoid Terry for they usually took the bus home together, but Steve's need to be alone, to think carefully, had increased and he couldn't stand any interruption.

His thoughts returned to Gary. Why had he been so anxious? Why was he always around? The words fell into a monotonous rhythm, beating away so hard Steve couldn't get rid of them.

He hadn't dared to walk by the river since Ed's death, but he knew exactly where he had drowned. Slowing down, he watched an old tyre twist and turn in the flood. The path was muddy and his black school shoes were filthy. He would have to find some grass to wipe them on or his mother would be furious.

Around the next corner, a bridge spanned the Don, with a narrow path underneath that was treacherously slippery.

Steve came to a momentary halt, gazing down at the fast-flowing water. Several times he and Ed had inched their way along the path, but with the river at a normal level there had been little danger and the adventure had fizzled out. Now, just one slip would send Steve into the torrent and he knew he wouldn't stand a chance of saving himself.

The urge to go under the bridge was so strong that it surprised him. Did he want to share another adventure with Ed? For old times' sake. But Ed was dead.

Why *should* he have to go under the bridge? Steve tried to shake off the terrible compulsion and had almost succeeded when he saw Ed in his mind's eye, almost as clearly as if he had been standing next to him on the muddy path, watching the swollen river with him. His presence was so real that when Steve half-turned he was amazed to find that he couldn't actually see him. All he could feel was the terrible urge.

Struggling hard not to give in, Steve still found his feet taking hesitant steps towards the bridge. Panic-stricken, he came to an uneasy standstill a few metres from the darkness under the bridge where the torrent thundered through. Then he remembered, with scant comfort, that he had had these inexplicable urges before, many years ago when he was a small child.

Steve recalled compelling himself to eat bacon rind and, later, to swallow part of a live worm. He shuddered at the thought of the stupidity of it all. For hours afterwards he had been sure he could feel the worm wriggling about inside his stomach. Yet Steve had been alone; no one had forced him on - and now, once again, Steve knew he *had* to edge his way under the bridge, however stupid and foolhardy he was being.

The river roared at him like a monstrous, angry serpent, and he saw a plywood box whirled by the current into the stonework of the bridge, smashing to pieces in a second. Sodden flakes of wood flew past him. Wasn't that a warning? But it was a warning Steve couldn't heed.

6

The torrent roared even louder in Steve's ears as he headed towards the bridge. The river was almost level with the path, swirling past as he began to edge along, his hands clawing at wet mould on the saturated bricks.

Steve still tried to fight against the urge, but he knew he was too weak, that he had to carry on until he reached the small sandy beach at the other end or fell into the muddy brown flood.

For a while the bricks under the bridge, damp and mouldy as they were, gave his hands some purchase, and Steve made slow progress clambering over debris that had been washed up in slippery piles, smelling the rank weed. This was an adventure, one of Ed's most dangerous, and for a split second Steve thought he could see him further up the narrow path, clinging on just as he was. Then he blinked and knew there was no one there at all.

He edged on, his dread returning, sure that he would slip at any moment, just as Ed had. Steve seemed to hear his voice all the time now. *I got drowned, didn't I?* Why had he given in to this dreadful urge? Just why?

Steve came to a halt as he reached an even larger pile of mud and broken wood that was blocking his way. He wasn't far from the sandy shore now and he could see it glinting slightly under a watery sun. Clinging to another mossy brick he began to kick the debris into the torrent where it was whisked away – just as he would be if he lost his footing.

Several times Steve felt himself slipping, but managed to save himself, finding a fingerhold and inching his way over the mud until he was within a metre of escape. But the path below him seemed even more treacherous than before and, what was worse, the river was beginning to surge over the edge. Water sloshed on to his shoes and his fingers grasped at the mossy bricks.

He *had* to make a dash for it.

He began to shuffle along as fast as he could, the torrent pulling at him, covering his shoes, cold water saturating his socks.

With a little whimper of fear, Steve forced himself on until he could see the strip of sandy shore and leapt to safety. But as he landed on the sand he fell and lay spread-eagled, gasping, looking up at the dark clouds that had covered the face of the sun.

Shivering violently, his uniform stained by the damp, muddy sand, Steve rose stiffly to his feet and glanced down at his broken fingernails, seeing the blood seeping through the lacerated skin. Why had he been such a fool? Why hadn't he been able to resist the urge? What was the matter with him? Still shaking, he began to run down the path towards home. But a few metres on he came to a shuddering halt as he heard the unmistakable sound of a telephone.

The insistent shrilling was coming from just round the corner where the path met the main road, and Steve began to run again, his damp clothes clinging horribly and, dread sweeping over him. As he turned the corner the telephone box came into sight, but the ringing abruptly stopped.

Then Steve noticed that someone was in there, but the glass was steamed-up and he couldn't make out who the bulky shadowy figure was.

He slowed down, but as he drew nearer the door opened and Gary emerged, glaring at him in sudden fury.

'You following me?' he asked belligerently.

'No way.'

They stood staring at each other in gathering hostility and suspicion.

'Push off!' said Gary.

Steve didn't move. 'I thought you might have answered a call.'

'What if I did?'

'Who was it?'

'Mate of mine.'

'Does he usually call you in a phone box?' asked Steve innocently.

'What's happened to you?' Gary demanded. 'Just taken a mud bath?'

'I fell over.'

Gary laughed unfeelingly. 'You're going to be in trouble with your mum, aren't you? What's she going to say when she claps her eyes on that school uniform then?'

Steve couldn't think of a sufficiently crushing reply and they walked on together in uneasy silence.

'Who was your mate?' He began to probe, knowing he sounded too casual.

'None of your business.' Gary paused. Then he changed his mind. 'If you must know it was this girl. Mary.'

'Mary who?'

'Goddard.'

'I don't know her.'

'She's not from our school.'

'So why is she calling you in a phone box?'

'My parents don't like her. We have to – to meet in secret. She calls me – and she – she –' Gary suddenly began to stutter slightly. 'We make a date on the phone.'

'So you can only see her on the quiet?'

'That kind of thing,' he replied vaguely.

Steve's mind was racing. Was Gary telling the truth or was it just a wind up? Did he have something to hide?

Leaving the sullen Gary at the corner of the street Steve ran home, deeply conscious of people staring at him and sniggering at his mud-caked appearance.

Then, just as the rain came down again, he saw a slight, skinny figure strolling along, seemingly in no hurry to avoid getting soaked. Ed often used to do that. He enjoyed walking in the rain. For a moment Steve became convinced that the figure in the old sweater and jeans was Ed. As he ran past he looked over his shoulder and illogical disappointment swept over him. It was a complete stranger – a girl of about his own age with very short hair – who was curiously returning his gaze.

Steve hurried on, feeling like an idiot.

'What do you think you've been doing?' Mum stood in the kitchen, looking at Steve in disgust. 'You've ruined your uniform.'

'I fell over. How's Gran?'

'They say she's comfortable. Have you been in a fight?' she demanded.

'No.'

'Then what –'

'I told you, I fell over.'

'You must have rolled about in the mud. Those clothes are ruined – and look at your shoes.'

Steve glanced down. He could see what she meant – they looked like a pair of muddy clogs.

'Go and have a shower and give me that uniform. I'll look at the damage and see what I can salvage, if anything.' His mother sighed. 'As if we haven't got enough trouble. I'd have thought you'd be more responsible at a time like this.' She sighed again. 'We'll go and see your gran after tea when you've done your homework.'

Steve ran up the stairs to the bathroom and slumped against the door. The whole episode with Gary had suddenly caught up with him and he felt very afraid.

When he had showered, had tea and listened to his mother complaining all over again, Steve went back up to his room, pretending he was going to hurry through his homework before going to the hospital. He felt exhausted after his battle under the bridge, but was determined not to fall asleep. Instead he wanted to try and rationalise what had been happening to him. Directly he lay on his bed, however, Steve's eyes began to close so he got up, went to the desk and started to write in his diary.

7

Thursday 5.25 PM

I was right - my weird day wasn't over! I can't believe what I've just done. I must have been crazy. But the urge to cross under the bridge was totally overpowering. I didn't feel in control of myself at all, it was really scary. And Mum's livid about my clothes. I've completely ruined my shoes! Never mind, I did it, and that's all that matters - Ed would have been proud of me. He enjoyed being crazy. He said it was what made life worth living. I'm still not sure what's going on though. I'm going to write it all down here - I need to make sense of everything.

'For' Something Strange Going On
1) The voice on the phone, breaking

through the static.

2) The voice calling me Stevie.

3) Saying something like 'I got drowned, didn't I?'

4) Gary following me and seeming scared. What's he scared of? He seems threatening too.

5) Uncontrollable urge to go under the bridge.

6) Who was Gary really talking to in the phone box? He looked scared when he saw me – scared and angry – and I'm not sure I believe in this girlfriend stuff. Who was he talking to?

'Against' Something Strange Going On

1) The computer problem at the exchange is making the phones go crazy.

2) I'm really upset about Ed. He's on my mind and that's what makes me think I can hear his voice on the phone when it's really in my imagination.

3) Gary isn't following me. He's

not scared and he isn't being any
more threatening than usual.
   4) Gary really does have a
girlfriend who calls him in the phone
box.
   I still can't make any sense of it.

Steve tilted his chair back against the wall and surveyed the two columns, slowly convincing himself that his grief for Ed had heightened his imagination. But there was still one aspect that continued to worry him. Gary.

He *wasn't* acting normally. He was watching him.

Steve paused, his head aching and confused.

Then an idea suddenly cut through his muddled thoughts, like a beam of sunshine after a storm, and the more Steve thought about it, the more sure he became.

He went back to his diary and wrote in capitals:

GARY THINKS I KNOW SOMETHING.

Know something about what, wondered Steve, and then realised it could only be about

Ed's death. How had he died? The coroner's verdict had been death by misadventure. Yet how could Ed have fallen into a calm river on a warm, sunny evening in early May. The rain had swollen the Don over the last few days, but when Ed drowned the water was calm. Of course, he wasn't a strong swimmer, but how had he tumbled in? OK, he was a daredevil, but he liked an audience.

Had Ed been unconscious when he went in? The pathologist at the inquest had said not, but nor had he found any bruising or other injuries.

So why did Gary think that he, Steve, knew something? What was there to know? What was Gary hiding?

He stared at his 'For' and 'Against' columns in bewilderment. The 'Against' *had* to be right. It was logical. But surely there was a certain logic to the 'For' column too.

Before Steve could contemplate any further, the telephone on the landing began to ring.

8

Thursday 5.58 PM

It's nearly time to visit Gran — I hope she's OK, I can't wait to see her. I wish I could talk to her about all this. There's not much evidence, and there could be an explanation for everything, but I've got to rely on my instincts and they tell me SOMETHING IS GOING ON. But what?

Watch this space for the next instalment...

Steve got to his feet, ran out on to the landing and grabbed the receiver, listening to the buzzing static. No voice came through, and he put the phone down, but directly he did so the ringing began again.

Unwillingly, he picked it up, but this time the static seemed louder and denser, like a thick hedge of thorns through which nothing could penetrate. As Steve replaced the phone again, his hand began to shake uncontrollably.

'What's going on?' Mr Parker was standing at the foot of the stairs, looking gaunt and tired.

'The phone was ringing.'

'Same problem?'

'Just static.'

'I've reported all this but they won't do a thing about it.'

His father sounded helpless and Steve wanted to reassure him but didn't know how.

'I mean, the phone could ring all night.'

They both stared at the receiver apprehensively while the sound seemed to hang in the air like an echo.

'They'll get it right, Dad.'

'Your mother reckons you've ruined those trousers and as for your shoes –'

'I'm sorry.'

'Do you think we're made of money?'

'No.'

'What were you up to?'

'I fell over.'

'Where?'

'On the path by the river.'

His father gazed up at him in consternation. 'What were you doing down there?'

Steve was silent.

'Come on –' Mr Parker's voice rose.

'I wanted to see where Ed drowned.'

There was a long silence. Then his father said slowly, 'That was pretty morbid, wasn't it?'

'I just wanted to –'

'Besides, the river's in flood now after all that heavy rain we've had and it was dangerous as well as being morbid.'

'I'm sorry, Dad. I couldn't understand how he'd drowned – how he'd slipped in.'

'We'll never know that.'

'Won't we?'

'We've had the coroner's report. Maybe he was larking about. You know what he was like.'

Steve shrugged.

'So how did you fall?' his father asked.

'Just slipped. But I wasn't larking about.'

'You'll have to put some of your pocket money towards those trousers. Mum's sending them to the dry cleaners to see if they can do something. She's not optimistic.'

'I'm sorry, Dad.'

'So am I.'

Then the phone began to ring again and Steve felt the fear churn, painful and nauseating.

*

As he picked up the receiver, his father climbed the stairs to stand beside him.

'Who's there?' Mr Parker asked hopefully.

'Nobody.' Steve passed over the phone. 'Can you hear anything?'

'Just static.'

'That's all we get.'

'Do you know, Steve, I'm beginning to feel I can't take much more of this. The phone rings and you expect someone to be on the other end, don't you? So it's a big let down when there's no one there.'

His father put the receiver back and started to walk down the stairs.

Then the ringing began again. 'Don't pick it up,' Mr Parker yelled, his voice sharp with tension. 'Just don't pick that thing up.'

But Steve already had. He listened again to the thick static but heard nothing more than that. He put the phone down hurriedly in case anything further happened.

'Static again?'

'Yes.'

His father looked at him closely. 'You look shaken up. Is it getting to you too?'

'Sort of.'

'Take it off the hook.'

Steve wasn't sure he wanted to do that. The constant ringing was terrible, but suddenly he had the bizarre thought that he *needed* the voice. Taking the receiver off the hook seemed the wrong thing to do.

'Should we do that?'

Mr Parker almost exploded with anger. 'Take the thing off!'

'The hospital might be trying to get through.'

'We're going there now!'

Steve kept his grip on the receiver as he tried to rationalise the situation yet again. The voice was in his mind, not on the phone. Wasn't it? But that was something that had to be proved and the more the telephone rang, the greater his chance of finding out the truth.

His father strode back up the stairs again, almost shouldering Steve aside. He pulled the receiver off the hook and left it hanging.

'I don't want to hear that ringing again. Not ever.'

'They'll have sorted out the computer problem soon.'

'I've gone off telephones.'

'Dad –'

His father's eyes blazed into his. 'If I find you've put the receiver back, you'll be in big trouble. Get me?'

Steve shrank back. Dad had never, ever spoken to him like that before.

'Do you get me?'

'I get you,' Steve said hurriedly.

'You sure?'

'You don't want me to put the phone back.'

Suddenly Steve felt he was going to lose control and either lash out at his father or start screaming. Desperate to escape, he ran back into his bedroom and slammed the door. He flopped down on the bed and gazed up at the ceiling.

Moments later there was a knock at the door. Steve ignored it.

After a few seconds, it came again.

'Who's there?'

'Dad.'

'Yeah?'

'I'm sorry.'

'It's OK.'

'I got worked up.'

'Sure.'

'Put the phone on again if you want.'

'I don't want.'

'What about the hospital?'

'As you said, we're going to see Gran in a minute, Dad.'

'That's right. You'd better get a jacket on. It's cold outside.' He sounded ashamed of himself.

Steve was grateful for the fact that the hospital would only allow one member of the family to see his grandmother at a time, each for five minute periods. Sandwiched between his mother and father's visits, he noticed Gran was looking completely drained as she sat up in bed, head against the pillow, her skin dry and papery. But her eyes were as sharp as ever and Steve soon found that her mind didn't seem to have been affected by the stroke.

'So what's the matter then?'

'I've been so worried about you.' He bent over to kiss Gran on her cheek.

'It's a minor stroke. Occupational hazard for old women like me. But tell me what's really the matter. You've got that preoccupied look. It's not just me, is it?'

She was right. Gran knew him through and through.

'You're not to upset yourself,' began Steve uncertainly, looking away.

'I will if you go on like this. Is it Ed?'

'Yes. But you're not to –'

'Will you shut up and listen to me?'

'Yes, Gran.'

'Sit on that chair.'

'I don't –'

'I told you to shut up.' Gran had her eyes fixed on him. 'Ed's death is a terrible tragedy for his parents and his friends and that means you. I'm an old woman. I've seen a lot of death and it doesn't affect me as it's affected you. I don't mean Ed. I mean death in general.'

'Yes, Gran.'

'But there's something else, isn't there?' Her eyes were like probes. 'You're worrying, not just grieving. What is it?'

'It's how he died,' Steve blurted out.

'He drowned.'

'On a quiet summer's evening?'

'Maybe he was larking about and fell in by mistake.'

'He wouldn't do that.'

'Maybe this was the one time he did.'

'Gran, I shouldn't be going on like this.'

Just then the nurse came in. 'Time's up,' she said.

'No, it's not,' snapped Gran. 'I'm talking to my grandson.'

'I'm afraid –'

'I'll go.' Steve got to his feet, feeling ashamed of himself. How could he be going on like this when she was so ill?

'You'll go when I'm good and ready.' Gran turned to the nurse. 'Give me two more minutes.' It was more like an order than a request.

The nurse nodded reluctantly. 'Just two, then.'

'Thank you.'

Gran waited until she had left and then said, 'Maybe Ed got a bang on the head.'

'How?'

'Walked into a tree? I don't know. What are you afraid of?' she asked, teasing it out of him, bit by bit.

'I'm afraid someone was with him.'

'I see.' She didn't seem in the least surprised. 'Then why didn't you say so before?'

'I was scared.'

'Do you know who was with him?'

Steve hesitated.

'Was it you?'

'No!'

'But you've got an idea.'

'Maybe.'

'Sure?'

'I can't say for sure.'

'All right.' Gran always knew when not to push too far. 'But sleep on it.'

'OK.'

'And if you decide you do know – do something about it. Promise me that, Stevie.'

'OK.'

'Really promise.' Suddenly the fatigue was showing in her face.

'I promise,' Steve said hurriedly, angry with himself for being so selfish.

'I still like to think I can help you. After all, you're my only grandson. Have you told Mum and Dad?'

'Not yet.'

'So it's our secret then. Until you make up your mind.'

'Yes, Gran.'

'So make it up quickly.'

Steve stood up and kissed her again. Her skin seemed cold and his anxiety returned. Suppose she died? What would he do without her?

'What took you so long?' asked his mother suspiciously as they sat in the white-painted, antiseptic-smelling corridor while Dad went to see the charge nurse.

'Gran wanted to talk.'

'What about?'

'The stroke.'

'It's only mild.'

'So she said.'

'Your gran shouldn't be living in that big house all on her own.'

'Try and stop her,' said Steve.

'She's frail now.'

He began to worry all over again.

Steve lay in bed, trying to drop off to sleep, but the threatening images kept slipping into his mind. Gran with her parchment skin. Gary in the phone box. The swirling, terrifying current of the river. Broken fingernails gripping the mildewed brick. Gary in the phone box. Static. The voice breaking through. Driftwood in the torrent. Gary in the phone box. Gran with her parchment skin.

Suddenly Steve heard the noise of static – at

least, he thought he did. He opened his eyes and looked round the room. Was that a stream of misty vapour coming under the door? Steve blinked, sure that he was half-dreaming as the mist thickened and the noise increased.

Shivering and feeling as if he could hardly breathe, he got out of bed. His feet were freezing cold on the normally warm bedroom carpet and the mist seemed to cling dankly to his ankles.

Somehow he managed to open his bedroom door, only to discover there was no mist on the landing, but the static was still loud. Steve gazed down at the dangling receiver just as his parents suddenly appeared at the bottom of the stairs.

'I don't believe it,' said his father. 'That phone's got a life of its own.'

'What are we going to do?' asked Mum, but without waiting for an answer she immediately added, 'There's only one thing we *can* do.'

'What's that?' demanded Mr Parker.

She ran lightly up the stairs and wrenched the telephone lead out of its socket. There was instant, solid, reassuring silence. Steve breathed a sigh of relief as his head began to clear.

'What about the hospital?' asked Dad.

'Listen to that wonderful silence,' said Mum. 'I

don't think we should ever have a telephone again.'

'What about the hospital?' repeated Dad, sounding like an automaton.

'I'll go and borrow next-door's mobile,' said Mum calmly. 'Freda won't mind. I'll call the ward and give them the number.'

'Suppose the mobile starts ringing on its own,' muttered Dad.

'What are you asking for, Charlie? A perfect world?'

'No. Just a quieter one.'

Too right, thought Steve. The silence seemed to spread over them like a cooling balm that deadened their raw nerves.

'At least we'll get some sleep tonight,' pronounced Dad.

Once back in his room, Steve picked up his diary and checked out his list again. But the words were blurred and meaningless.

9

Friday, 16th

I didn't dream last night, thank goodness. In fact, I slept so well I'm about to be late for school, but I wanted to write a brief morning entry because I feel so much better. All the things that have happened don't seem so dark and mysterious any more. In fact, I'm pretty sure that what happened was all in my mind.

More later...

Steve was so late he had to rush off to school without any breakfast, but he didn't really care for this morning he felt much safer, more a part of the ordinary, everyday world. Somehow, in ripping the telephone from its socket, Mum had demonstrated how strong and resourceful she was. Why couldn't he and Dad have taken such decisive action? Her solution had been so simple.

As Steve ran along the pavement towards school, he remembered how, when he was much younger, he had relied on his mother to reassure him – in particular about the cracks in his bedroom ceiling which seemed so threatening when he switched off the light, becoming shadowy witches and goblins and monsters, leering down at him, making horrible noises.

Mum would rush in when he cried out, waving her feather duster at the phantoms and shouting, 'Get off the ceiling, you lot!' Within seconds they were gone and they didn't dare to reappear all night.

'You're just winding up that boy's imagination,' Steve had once overheard his father saying. 'Making him believe in things that don't exist.'

But whenever Steve had called for her in the night, Mum had always appeared with her feather duster to flick the demons away.

A telephone was ringing as he walked past the school reception and Steve whipped round, realising it was the students' pay-phone . That's odd, he thought, it was only meant to be used for outgoing calls. But now someone was dialling in, and the ringing was sharp and clear and persistent.

Mum, you've got to unplug the phone at school as well. Mum, you've got to do something. Then Steve chastised himself for being such a wimp.

The pay-phone must be ringing because there was a fault at the exchange – it was as simple as that. But Steve felt that his world had become circular, for each time he seemed to solve a problem, something happened to open it up all over again.

He looked round for Mrs Milford, but the school office was empty. Maybe she was with the head teacher, out of range of the phone.

Still hesitating, Steve waited. He was late and would have to sign in. If he went on into school without doing so he'd get into trouble, but there was still no sign of Mrs Milford. Would she suddenly emerge with a feather duster and flick the demons away for him? Steve didn't think so.

What was he going to do? He couldn't let the phone go on ringing like this; the sharp, urgent tone was beginning to get to him.

Nervously, he went over to the pay-phone and lifted the receiver, only to find the static was as loud and penetrating as before. Steve listened hard, his heart hammering, sweat beginning to trickle into his eyes. Then the painful sound began to recede, and gradually it thinned until he could hear something which at first he couldn't identify, but he knew wasn't a voice. Suddenly recognition came with a resounding shock as Steve realised he was listening to the sound of water. Not a tap or a shower, but the gentle lapping of a river on a grassy bank.

Then the static returned.

'What's the matter, Steven?'

He had just managed to replace the receiver when Mrs Milford arrived with a pile of folders. Just behind her, lurking near the lockers, was the all too familiar and unsettling figure of Gary, obviously eavesdropping. Why did he always turn up when there was a telephone ringing?

'Nothing, miss.'

'You can't receive incoming calls on the students' pay-phone. You should know that. So what were you doing?'

Steve was at a complete loss for words. Had she been spying on him too, just like Gary?

'Well?'

'I was making a call.'

'Who were you phoning?'

'My mother.'

'And?'

'She wasn't in.'

'Was it about your grandmother? Is she worse?' Mrs Milford suddenly remembered Steve's family crisis.

'No. She's better, I think.'

'Back home?'

'Not yet.'

'I'm so sorry.'

There was a long awkward silence during which Gary pretended to be studying a notice board.

'Are you all right?' Mrs Milford looked concerned. 'You're sweating again. There's an awful lot of this summer flu about –'

'I feel fine.' Steve didn't want to be sent home where he would be alone with the phone.

'Don't you think you should see the nurse?'

'No thank you, miss.'

Mrs Milford sighed and then whipped round. 'Gary Jenkins,' she yelled, and Steve wondered if she had an additional eye in the back of her head. 'What do you think you're doing?'

'Reading the notices, miss.'

'Rubbish! You were listening to my conversation with Steven Parker.'

A little crowd of curious bystanders was gathering now, hoping for trouble, but Mrs Milford didn't seem to notice them.

'I'm waiting for an answer.'

'Er –' Gary began haltingly.

'That's not an answer. Come on, why were you listening? What kind of stupid game are you playing?'

'I'm not playing a game, miss.'

Mrs Milford sighed and the little crowd rustled expectantly and then went quiet.

'Listen, Gary, every time I see Steven I see you. It's got to stop. Why are you following him?'

'I'm not, miss.'

'Can you shed any more light on this, Steven?'

'No, miss.'

'I know something's going on.' Mrs Milford walked slowly back into the reception office, looking bemused. Steve was sorry to see her go.

'What's happening?' demanded Gary. He looked badly rattled as Steve passed him on the way to his locker.

'Nothing.' He stuck to his usual denial.

'What is it?'

'I don't know what you're on about,' said Steve. 'Why don't you push off?'

Gary suddenly lost control. He grabbed Steve by the shoulders, swung him round and rammed him hard up against the lockers.

'What's going on?' he whispered, his pudgy features contorted in fury, his breath smelling sharply of stale onions. 'Who was on the phone?' Gary had his hands round Steve's throat now and his thumbs were pressing on his windpipe.

'Let go!' croaked Steve, but he knew that however hard he struggled, Gary's grip would only get tighter.

'Who was on the phone?'

'No one.'

'Tell me!' Gary increased the pressure and Steve began to gasp for breath.

'There's a fault at the exchange,' he managed to get out. 'You should know that. The phones just keep ringing.' He could hardly breathe and was seeing a reddish dark mist, which got denser as Gary continued to squeeze.

One or two pupils hurried past, but no one

stopped to help Steve. Gary was too much feared.

'Who was on the phone?' he repeated.

'Why do you want to know?' Steve rasped.

Suddenly Terry arrived, grabbing Gary round the neck and tripping him up. They fell to the floor with Terry on top, fist upraised.

'Stop that, you two!' shouted Mr James, the deputy head, as he strode down the corridor towards them. 'Get up!'

Slowly, they rose to their feet.

'It wasn't Terry's fault,' said Steve, his voice hoarse and breathless. 'Gary attacked me.'

'That's right,' yelled someone. 'He went psycho.'

'He got me round the throat. He was going to strangle me.'

'He's a right nutter,' observed Terry.

'You're getting to be a very nasty sort of bully, aren't you, Gary?' said Mr James contemptuously.

'He said something about my dad!'

'Liar!' shouted Steve and Terry together.

'On my mother's life, he did,' muttered Gary, his eyes blank, brow furrowed, knowing he was trapped.

'Come to my office, Gary. I want a word with you.'

'What about?' he replied, desperately playing for time.

'I'm going to sort out your attitude problem once and for all,' said Mr James. 'Now get moving.'

Another thunderstorm was building up as Steve and Terry strolled across the playground. Dark clouds had again shut out the sun and the sullen heat was oppressive. Steve's throat hurt and he wished Mr James had sent him to the nurse so he didn't have to have the inevitable conversation with Terry. Then he felt ashamed. Without Terry's intervention, Gary could have done some serious damage. But what had got him into such a rage in the first place?

'Thanks for what you did, Tel,' said Steve.

'I've always wanted to have a go at that big ox. I'd like to thank you, Steve Parker, for giving me the chance.'

He grinned and punched him on the arm, but looked puzzled when Steve didn't grin back.

'What's up then?' Terry seemed almost as curious as Gary and just as demanding. Why can't they all leave me alone, thought Steve. I can't stand it much longer.

'Nothing,' he said hurriedly.

'Can't you handle Gary?'

'He jumped me. I didn't have a chance.'

Terry nodded. There was clearly something else on his mind.

'You've been avoiding me, haven't you?' He sounded suddenly and uncharacteristically vulnerable.

'Have I?' Steve chose to be evasive.

'I want to help.'

'I know you do.'

'If it's not that big ox, Gary, bugging you, then who is it? Ed?'

Steve knew he couldn't take much more and suddenly let go. He just had to confide in someone. 'I keep seeing him.'

'Where?' Terry looked mystified.

'Up here.' He tapped his forehead. 'Where do you think?'

'You were close, weren't you?'

'Sort of.'

'Didn't Ed go around with Gary too?'

'A bit.'

'Why was that?'

'I dunno.'

Terry paused. 'Do you reckon Gary had a hold over Ed then?'

'I don't know.' Steve had never known Terry to be so perceptive. Could he have underestimated him? He glanced at Terry with a new respect.

'I saw them once, talking out on the field. Ed looked weird.'

'What sort of weird?'

'Scared weird.' Terry paused expectantly, but Steve said nothing. 'So you don't know –'

'Don't know what?'

'What was going on.'

'Haven't a clue.'

There was a long silence as they continued across the playing field; the thunder growled in the distance and Steve's head throbbed. For a moment he felt as if he was going to pass out. Then the giddiness cleared.

'What do you reckon then?' Steve felt momentarily dependent on Terry. He needed someone to tell him if he was going crazy or not. Although he hadn't dared talk about the calls for fear of being sent up, at least he could discuss Gary. 'You only saw them once?'

'Yeah.'

Steve's desire to confide faded again, as if something had blocked his mind, and he stared ahead blankly.

'You can't get him out of your mind then,' Terry prodded.

'What about the match tomorrow?' Steve asked desperately.

'We'll take them, if –' Terry began, and then broke off.

'If what?'

'You're on form.'

Steve nodded, trying to show enthusiasm, but only feeling a total lack of interest. What did the stupid match matter? All he could think about was the phone and the voice he couldn't tell anyone about.

10

Friday 4.30 PM

Thank goodness Friday is over. I'm more confused than ever and I'm scared too. I'm sure now that Gary had some hold over Ed - he must have done. I could never work out what they had in common and what their friendship was based on. If Gary did have a hold over Ed then there could be a connection between him and Ed drowning. I need to get to the bottom of this, for Ed's sake.

That evening, Steve's grandmother was discharged from hospital and came to stay with Steve and his parents, on the strict understanding that 'it wouldn't be for long'. He knew she valued her independence too much to want to be looked after. But when Gran arrived, she was so tired that she went straight to bed.

Meanwhile, the telephone was still unplugged, rather as if a demon had been temporarily subdued.

It was the night before the match and Steve couldn't sleep at all. Every time he tried to switch off, he heard the sound of the lapping river. Then, as he closed his eyes, the lapping became a torrent.

Eventually, he drifted off, tossing and turning, the sound of a raging flood in his ears and slowly, towards dawn, Steve began to dream. He was running along the path by the river, pursued by dozens of black telephones that slid along the ground after him, their leads slithering along like snakes. Every time he turned to look at them Steve saw little red tongues wriggling in the mouthpieces.

He woke gasping, thrashing about, not knowing where he was, until he saw the cracks in his bedroom ceiling. As usual, they looked hostile, and Steve wished he was years younger, still able to call out for his mother.

His limbs felt as heavy as lead and he was exhausted. How was he going to be any good on the field? For a while Steve contemplated feigning illness. Then he dragged himself out of bed, knowing he could never face himself if he couldn't face the day.

Steve stood in the goal-mouth, watching the ball, his mouth dry, his head aching. He knew he wasn't on form and the thundery heat seemed stifling.

A straggle of spectators, largely parents, were cheering on the game, some of them shouting instructions that only confused the players. The score was two-all and they were now into extra time. Steve had already saved a couple of goals, but because he was feeling so lousy, the saves were more by luck than judgement.

The Wanderers' striker was running up the field, expertly dribbling the ball, eyes set on the goal. Steve tried hard to concentrate, but as he came nearer, a mobile telephone suddenly began to ring. He glanced at the crowd, but no one seemed to have noticed, and although the ringing became shrill and persistent no one answered.

He heard shouting, and whipped round to see the Wanderers' striker within metres of him. But now the ringing was even louder, freezing

Steve's will, blocking his mind.

The striker wore a fixed and mocking grin, as if he knew Steve was distracted. There was a dull thud of boot on leather and Steve leapt up, only to see the ball land in the back of the net.

A dull groan went up from the home side and the ringing stopped as suddenly as it had begun.

Once again Steve gazed in bewilderment at the crowd, for no one seemed to be speaking into a mobile. Had the caller rung off? But why hadn't the owner answered? To let a mobile ring for so long near the goal was sabotage. It shouldn't have been allowed. He should appeal to the ref.

Then Steve saw a woman hurrying away with two young children, one of whom was grinning. The woman was grabbing something out of the child's hand and shoving it back in her handbag, but Steve was too far away to see exactly what it was. She seemed to be angry and he wondered if her child had somehow got hold of her mobile and refused to give it up. Steve supposed it was just possible.

He gazed round at the disappointed faces of his team mates, feeling deeply ashamed. He'd lost concentration and let them all down. Terry was shaking his head, looking puzzled and fed up.

As the teams walked off the pitch, Steve desperately apologised to every player on his side. They all shrugged and said it was just bad luck, but he knew how disappointed they were at the way he had failed to make such an easy save.

'I'm really sorry,' Steve said yet again, this time to Mick Jordan, the manager.

'Stop going on!' Mick was tall and thin with an ironic sense of humour. He was tough on his players but also generous. When they had won the shield last summer, Mick had taken the whole team to McDonalds. 'Everyone has an off-day,' he reassured Steve.

'I blew it.'

'So have I. Dozens of times. Forget it. No one's worried.' Mick paused awkwardly, and Steve knew what was coming. 'Hear you had a loss like.'

'Yeah.'

'Best mate?'

'Sort of.'

'No wonder you're off form. If you ever want to talk about it –'

'I'm OK.'

'All right then.' Mick had done his bit. 'Go

and have a shower.' He dug in his pocket and pulled out a chocolate bar. 'And get stuck into that.'

Steve suddenly glimpsed a burly figure hurrying away from the pitch, and with a sharp shock recognised Gary's retreating back. What was he doing here? He had never come to watch the team play before. So why had he come today? To keep him under surveillance?

'What's the matter?' Mick was all concern again. 'You look as if you've seen a ghost!'

'Just a mate.'

Mick swung round. 'Isn't that Gary Jenkins over there?'

'You know him?' Steve was surprised.

'He used to be in the junior league, years back. I'd still recognise him anywhere.'

'Was he any good?'

'Not bad. But when he started to put on weight he ran out of puff.' Mick paused. 'Got into some bad company too. You'd better watch out for him.'

'Thanks.' Steve began to jog back to the changing room where Terry was waiting for him.

'What you got there?'

'What does it look like?'

'Do we all get chocolate if we mess up?' Terry looked at Steve greedily. 'Give us a bit.'

Steve broke off a few squares for him.

'Wasn't that Gary on the touchline? Was he putting you off?' Terry gazed at him curiously.

Steve shook his head. 'I didn't see him till after the match.'

'What's he doing here then?'

'Dunno.'

'Maybe he's keeping an eye on you.'

'What for?'

'That's what I'd like to know,' said Terry pointedly.

For a moment Steve almost cracked, desperate to tell him about the mobile. But he changed his mind. Terry wouldn't believe him. Terry was too full of common sense.

Steve waited by the bus stop. The sky was steel grey and the Saturday afternoon street was practically empty of pedestrians, as if they had all taken shelter from the heat. Even the traffic was light, rattling past in a cloud of dust and exhaust fumes.

He felt heavy and dull, his head thumping

with pain, and he wondered if he was really sickening for something.

As the bus rounded the corner Steve could see with relief that it was almost empty. He climbed the stairs to find a cooler spot by an open window and saw there was only one other passenger, a businessman with a briefcase, sitting right up at the front.

Then, just as the bus lurched forward, he heard a clattering sound as someone scrambled on at the last minute and came running up the stairs, panting and gasping.

Steve had sat himself a few rows behind the businessman and stared determinedly out of the window, but not before he had half turned to glimpse Gary. He sat down heavily beside him, smelling of sweat.

'Fancy seeing you.'

'What do you want?' Steve was ungracious.

'Didn't you see me at the match?'

'What do you want?' Steve repeated, feeling like a zombie, completely emotionless, not even afraid.

'You blew the game.'

'Thanks.'

'Was Mick mad?'

'He stayed quite sane actually.'

'Something on your mind?' Gary looked at him almost triumphantly.

'I don't think so. What did *you* come to the match for?'

'I came to see you.'

Steve felt a stab of fear. 'Why did you do that?'

'In case the phone rang.' Gary giggled and Steve wondered if it had been him playing with the mobile. Could he have been trying to wind him up? 'Didn't I hear a ringing sound?' Gary asked, with suspicious curiosity.

'Not in the middle of a match,' said Steve firmly. 'Why didn't you stay afterwards?'

'Some of the guys in the team don't like me.'

'I wonder why?'

As he spoke a phone began to ring and for a moment Steve wondered if it was only ringing in his imagination.

Then he saw the businessman pulling his mobile out of his briefcase.

Steve froze and he could feel Gary rigid and tense beside him.

'I can't hear a word. There's a buzzing sound on the line. Who? Who do you want to speak to?' There was a slight pause. 'I've never heard of him. What? I told you, I've never heard of Gary Jenkins. Who is he? And who's this calling?'

Steve felt hot and cold at the same time, as if he had a fever. Beside him, Gary leant forward, pressed his hands pressed to his forehead and rocked himself to and fro.

Meanwhile, the businessman was rapidly losing his temper. 'What is all this rubbish? I can't hear you. There's too much crackling. You must have got the wrong number.' He switched off the phone, and with an irritable grunt shoved it into his pocket.

The bus began to slow down. Steve felt as if he couldn't move, that he was stuck to his seat, but desperate to escape he forced himself out of his inertia, and stood up. He pushed past Gary, ran the length of the double-decker and clattered down the stairs.

'Stop!' yelled Gary, getting to his feet.

The businessman looked back in further irritation as Gary thundered towards the staircase. Then his mobile began to ring again. Gary hovered at the top of the staircase, listening.

'Look. I haven't got time for kids' games,' he barked into the mouthpiece. 'What is this? Some kind of wind up? Wait a minute. Is that you, Emily? I'm so sorry –'

Reassured, Gary ran down the staircase and jumped off the bus.

'I want to talk,' he yelled after Steve's retreating figure, now in the distance, running beside the fast-flowing river towards the bridge.

11

Steve felt confused and uneasy. What was he doing, running back this way? He had had to get off the bus, to get away from Gary, and that was understandable. Surely it was just a coincidence that the bus stop had been near the river. But why hadn't he run in the opposite direction? Was it because Gary was close behind him?

'Give me a break,' muttered Steve to himself. 'Just give me a break.'

As he ran on, Steve was suddenly sure he could hear ringing in the distance, and glancing back saw Gary still puffing his way towards him past the telephone box opposite the bus stop.

Gary looked over his shoulder at the telephone and then put on a spurt, narrowing the distance between them as Steve ran alongside the fast-flowing river that was still flooding the path. As he splashed on, Steve wondered yet again why he didn't branch away over the meadows. But something was compelling him to stay on the path; it was as if he had no will of his own left at all.

'Let go, Ed,' Steve muttered to himself, using the name for the first time. 'You've got to let go. You don't want me to drown too, do you?' Steve shivered inside – why had he said that?

The ringing grew fainter and the gap between Steve and Gary widened. A couple of swans paddled past, used now to the flood stream, taking advantage of the current.

Steve didn't want to go on but he couldn't turn back. Suddenly panic surged through him and he came to an abrupt halt. What was the long black thing snaking towards him? Could it be a telephone receiver, or the angry head of a cobra?

Steve gazed at it with creeping horror, unable to decide whether he was watching an enormous black snake or, even more unbelievably, a telephone receiver travelling towards him on an incredibly long lead.

He shut his eyes against the idea, and when he opened them again Steve gasped with relief as he realised he was staring at the withered remains of a long creeper that had been torn from a tree. He let out a huge sigh. What was the matter with him? He was getting so anxious that he was almost hallucinating.

Suddenly aware that Gary should have caught up by now, Steve turned round to see what had happened to him. Rain was lashing down now, and through the streaming deluge he heard a splash and a desperate cry for help.

'Help me, Steve! You've got to help me.'

Steve stared down at the torrent as Gary swirled past him, hurtling towards the bridge. Somehow he had slipped in. Just like Ed had.

'I can't swim!' he screamed and went under.

Steve continued to gaze down at the fast-flowing Don as if he was watching a film, completely detached from the real situation. He waited for Gary to come up again. But he didn't. Could he have got caught up with some obstruction below the surface? The answer seemed academic, as if he was filling in an exam paper: How many ways can Gary drown? Answer on one side of the page only.

Steve scanned the water, looking for signs of life. Suddenly a hand emerged from below the surface as if desperately waving and then Gary's head appeared, his mouth wide open, gasping and spluttering. Steve knew he should help him, but once again he felt rooted to the spot, unable to shake off the feeling that he was being held there against his will.

Then, like an elastic band pulled too tight, something snapped in Steve's mind and without thinking he ran to the swollen river and dived in.

Gary went under again and came up panicking, thrashing his arms about all over the place and punching at Steve as he tried to put him into a life-saving position.

'You'll drown me!' he shrieked.

The roar of the river in flood thundered in Steve's ears as they were pulled under the bridge, spinning along at high speed.

'You're drowning yourself!' Steve shouted.

Gary suddenly went limp, as if he had given up, and after a long struggle Steve managed to drag him on to his back, support his head and kick out towards the bank. For a while he thought he might get there, but the current proved too strong and they were both swept into a narrow section of the river that ran past some abandoned industrial buildings, gaunt under the rain-lashed sky.

Eventually Steve saw an inlet that led between the warehouses. If he could only steer

Gary in that direction and kick out harder with his legs, they might just make it.

Steve struck out. At first Gary's weight and the strength of the current seemed too strong for him, but gradually he began to make a little headway.

As he did so, Steve saw something black and twisted across the mouth of the inlet. What was it? A snake? A telephone on a long lead? For a moment his imagination got the better of him, but then he realised that it was just a length of metal piping that was straddling the creek. If only he could fight against the current he might be able to grab it. But what was he going to do with Gary?

With an enormous effort, Steve managed to pull him into the inlet as if towing a stranded whale. The pipe was above them now, corroded by rust, and he wondered if it would take both their weights. He reached up and managed to get a hand-hold, wrenching his shoulder in the process, while Gary had woken up and was splashing wildly, his legs now locked round Steve's, a dead weight that threatened to drag them both down.

'Reach up, you idiot!' he yelled, and in

desperation Gary also grabbed at the pipe. There was a rending sound and a horrible crack, but the pipe held.

'What do we do now?' gasped Gary.

'We'll have to get across to the other side.'

'I can't do that.' He was shivering violently.

'You've got to. Follow me.'

'I haven't got the strength in my wrists!'

Steve ignored him and slowly began to swing along the pipe with his hands until he reached a ruined quay that was half broken away. Turning, he saw to his amazement that Gary was following, his eyes wild with panic, and as Steve jumped down to the pitted concrete he yelled, 'Come on, Gary. You can do it.'

Gary began to pull himself along even more frantically than before, just making it to the crumbling quayside as one section of the pipe began to sag. He reached up a desperate arm which Steve grabbed, and for a moment he was sure that they were both going to fall into the creek again where they would surely be swept back into the current of the main stream. Luckily, Gary managed to find some purchase with his feet on the scarred side of the quay, and with Steve's help he scrambled up to safety.

Gasping for breath, Gary and Steve stood there in the pouring rain, gazing into each other's eyes, shivering so violently that they were barely in control of their limbs.

'We need to get dry,' said Steve shakily.

'How?'

They gazed around at the derelict quay and its decaying buildings. Then Steve saw an old shed that at least had a roof and turned towards the darkness of the open doorway. Gary followed.

12

As Steve's eyes got used to the gloom, he saw a pile of old sacks in a corner. He tested them and found they were bone dry and, in the circumstances, as welcoming as the most luxurious of beds.

'Get under these,' Steve suggested.

'They're filthy,' objected Gary.

'We'll catch pneumonia if we don't. Besides –'

'Besides what?'

'I want to talk.'

'What about?' Gary was immediately suspicious.

'Ed.'

Gary hesitated and Steve wondered if he was going to run off. But instead, he grabbed at a couple of sacks, sat down and pulled them around him. Steve did the same and they half-sat, half-lay until their shivering slowly subsided.

Suddenly, from somewhere behind them, something scuttled across the floor and Gary squealed, 'That's a rat!'

Steve shrugged. 'There's worse things –'

'You saved my life,' Gary muttered, as if he was only just realising the extent of what had happened.

'So tell me about Ed.' Steve seized his chance.

'I'll try.'

Steve gazed at Gary curiously. He never gave a straight answer to anyone. Was this going to be a first?

'But you mustn't grass me up.'

'I can't guarantee that,' said Steve bleakly.

There was a long silence between them until Steve repeated, 'Tell me about Ed.'

Gary hesitated. 'He slipped and fell in.'

Is that all? The phrase beat in Steve's head mockingly. *He slipped and fell in. He slipped and...*

'Slipped? How did he slip?'

'He was climbing a tree.'

Steve couldn't remember a tree that overhung the water. 'Which tree?' he asked.

Gary didn't reply, but carried on rather uncertainly, 'The branch snapped and Ed went in.'

'So why didn't you get him out?'

'I can't swim.'

'You mean you stood and watched him drown?' Steve gazed at Gary incredulously.

'Ed got…got swept downstream and I couldn't keep up with him.'

In one way, his explanation sounded too neat; in another Steve supposed Gary could be telling the truth.

'What happened next?'

'He went under and didn't come up again.'

'Did you call for help?'

'There wasn't anyone else around.'

'So what did you do?' snapped Steve, beginning to shiver again, hugging the sacks around him.

'I wanted to get help –' Gary was very agitated now, his fingers plucking repeatedly at the sacks. 'But I was scared of being blamed.'

'So?'

'So I couldn't risk being spotted.' Gary stared at Steve as if he was thinking hard. 'I saw this old lady walking her dog, but she'd have been useless and anyway she'd have told everyone I was there at the time. So I hid till she went past me. By then it would have been too late for Ed and I was too scared to tell anyone in case they thought I'd had something to do with it.'

Steve was still trying to adjust himself to what had happened, what *might* have happened.

Gary's face was devoid of any expression. He was giving nothing away. But none of what he had just said really rang true. *Rang* true? Why did he have to think about the phones at a time like this? Steve felt cold inside.

'I didn't know what to do,' said Gary.

'There's more, isn't there? There's got to be more.'

'There isn't.'

'And the next morning?'

'I felt terrible all night. But I didn't know for sure until I went to school.'

'And then?'

'I heard he was dead. I heard he'd drowned.' Gary began to give a series of dry, harsh sobs. 'It wasn't my fault. There was nothing I could do. I'm sorry. Really sorry.'

'You could have rung the police.'

Gary didn't reply and Steve stared hard into his crumpled face, feeling completely numb, neither hating nor condemning him. He was just so shattered that anyone, even Gary, could let someone drown – do nothing about it whatsoever.

Gary's sobs increased, as if he was trying to insist that Steve believe him.

'Did you know Ed couldn't swim?' Steve asked.

'It wasn't my fault he climbed the tree. He fell,' Gary repeated. 'He fell into the river and I was too scared to tell anyone. I'm sorry. I didn't want him to drown.'

Slowly a slither of rage began to eat into Steve's numbness. 'You could be in real trouble.'

'You won't tell?' Gary was on his knees now, pulling away the sacks, whining, pleading.

'Why not?'

'If you do, I'll beat you up.'

Steve laughed, his rage deepening as he remembered how Gary had been watching him for so long, eavesdropping on his calls and trying to work out what, if anything, he knew. Then, on the bus, the call had finally come for him personally. Is that why he was trying to make this so-called confession?

'Why were you scared by the phones ringing?' demanded Steve.

'Scared?' Gary repeated. 'I don't know what you mean.'

But Steve could see the shifting fear in his eyes.

'Did you hear Ed?' he asked quietly, trying to control his anger.

'Before he got drowned do you mean?'

Steve hesitated. 'Did you hear Ed on the phone *after* he was dead?'

'What are you on about? Are you off your trolley?'

'What about the call on that mobile just now? It was for you, wasn't it? Did Ed want to speak to you? Is that why you got scared and told me all this – so he'd leave you alone?'

'You are crazy.'

'Then why tell me?'

'I owed you, you just saved my life and I needed to talk to someone.' Gary paused and then looked away. 'Now I know what it's like to drown…' He sounded almost convincing.

'I'm going to the police.' Steve stood up. 'They'll get the truth out of you.'

'I've told you the truth.'

'Then you've got nothing to worry about.'

They were both standing up now, and Steve's rage faltered for a moment as he wondered if he could handle Gary. Last time he had been taken by surprise, but now he was ready. A shaft of watery sunshine filtered in through the open door and he realised the rain had stopped.

'Please, Steve. Don't tell anyone about this. I lost my nerve, that's all.' Gary was pleading more desperately than ever.

'You lost Ed.'

'I know he was a mate of yours –'

'And yours. What's more, he had a mum and dad and a kid sister –'

'It wasn't my fault he climbed the tree. I couldn't stop him.' Gary was back to square one. 'I told you how sorry I am.'

'If you'd have told someone, even that old lady, I might have believed you,' said Steve angrily.

'I was scared.'

'Sure,' said Steve.

Gary turned to the door, his fists clenched. 'I'm going home.'

'You're not going anywhere unless it's the police station, and I'm coming with you.'

'Get out of my way.'

'No chance.'

They moved closer to one another, each waiting for the other to strike the first blow.

Suddenly Gary took a swing at Steve, but as he dodged clear, a fast follow-up punch landed squarely in his stomach.

Steve went down gasping, knees drawn up, fighting for breath.

'Let that be a warning,' yelled Gary as he ran past him into the gathering sunshine. 'A final warning.'

Steve dripped his way home, filthy and wringing wet, hoping to avoid the curious stares of passers-by this time by keeping to the less frequented roads. Then, to his acute embarrassment, he saw a couple of girls from the year above walking towards him, arm-in-arm, giggling at some private joke. They'll have an even bigger laugh when they clap eyes on me, Steve thought, but there was no way of avoiding them, particularly as the pavement opposite was closed for repairs. He began to jog, but as he tried to pass them, the girls blocked his path.

Steve had always feared them for they unfailingly went out of their way to try and humiliate boys. And they were often successful. Anne-Marie was tall and good looking with long blond hair, while Ronelle was slightly shorter and less willowy, her dark hair short and sleek. Now they were both grinning, pleased to have chanced upon such a likely victim.

'You're a bit on the mucky side,' said Ronelle.

'A bit of a mucky duck,' added Anne-Marie.

'Someone throw you in a river then? What's your mum going to say? I bet she'll go bananas.'

'I've been playing football,' Steve lied stupidly, his mind having gone completely blank.

'In your ordinary clothes?' asked Ronelle. 'Forgot to take your sports kit, did you? Now that wasn't a very clever thing to do. Bit hard on your mum, isn't it?'

Anne-Marie rubbed some dirt off Steve's cheek. 'Can you teach me to play football?'

Steve felt himself going crimson.

'I do believe he's blushing,' said Ronelle maliciously.

As she spoke, the telephone in the box on the corner of the street began to ring.

'That's odd,' said Ronelle.

'There's a fault at the exchange,' stammered Steve. 'The phones ring all the time, but there's no one at the other end.'

'Suppose there is this time?' Anne-Marie was curious, and he could see that she was losing interest in humiliating him.

'Don't bother,' Steve advised, as she ran over to the box and went inside.

'Never a dull moment, is there?' commented Ronelle.

Anne-Marie picked up the receiver, listening intently, looking as if she was throwing in the odd question. Steve became increasingly uneasy.

'Who's she talking to?' demanded Ronelle, her curiosity mounting.

'Why ask me?'

'She doesn't look too happy now, does she?'

They watched Anne-Marie's intent, alarmed expression. When she put down the receiver, she stood in the box for a while and then slowly came out.

'What's going on?' demanded Ronelle.

'I dunno.'

'What do you mean?' asked Steve anxiously.

'There was this voice, a male voice, but the line was crackling and sometimes I couldn't hear it at all.'

'What did he say?' asked Ronelle.

'I think the voice asked for Steve Parker.' Anne-Marie turned on Steve. 'What is this? Some kind of wind up?'

'Oh, that.' He was thinking quickly.

'What do you mean, "Oh, that"?' she snapped.

'Didn't you hear about it on the grapevine at school?'

'Hear what?' She was hungry for information.

'About the hoax.'

'What hoax?'

'That voice asking for me. Some crazy kid at school. He's called teachers, the school secretary…even the caretaker.'

'Wait a minute,' cautioned Ronelle. 'Aren't you the one who's had a bit of a tragedy recently?' Like Mrs Milford, she suddenly became warm and compassionate. 'That kid who drowned. He was a mate of yours, wasn't he?'

'Yeah. He was a mate all right.'

'Is this kid at school trying to wind you up?'

'What's that got to do with Ed?'

'I don't know, but if someone's winding you up at a time like this I'll have his guts.'

'So will I,' said Anne-Marie, completely in agreement with Ronelle. 'It's a filthy trick.'

'I know it is,' Steve agreed, seeing a way through.

'This kid's phone bill must be enormous,' observed Ronelle with some satisfaction.

'Does he always ask for you?' demanded Anne-Marie. The girls were gazing at him with increasing sympathy and Steve felt more in control.

'Always.'

'You're sure you don't know who it is?'

'I haven't got a clue.'

'This kid got something against you?'

'I suppose so.'

Anne-Marie touched his wet sleeve. 'Have you really been playing football?'

'Of course I have.'

'I don't believe you.'

For a moment Steve almost broke down and told Anne-Marie and Ronelle everything. He needed support. Anyone's support.

Then the phone began to ring again, and Steve pushed his way past the girls, breaking into a run, heading for home.

13

Saturday, 17th

There's almost too much to write down. My head is buzzing with it all and I don't know where to begin. I know Gary's involved - at least he's admitted that much, but I don't think he's told me everything. I can't believe what he did - how could he have left Ed to drown like that? Not made the slightest attempt to get help. I need Gary to tell me the whole truth - there's more, I'm sure of it. But I'm really scared - I know too much and if it wasn't for me, he'd be able to hide the truth for ever...

Steve's tea was on the kitchen table with a note from his parents saying they had gone to an early film and that their next-door neighbour, Mrs Fenton, was upstairs looking after Gran.

He took a shower, scrubbing off all trace of the clinging mud, and put on some clean jeans and a T-shirt, dumping his dirty clothes in the washing machine. Mum would be furious – this was the second lot of clothes he'd ruined in a week – but if she knew the reason she'd understand. Maybe she soon would. He had a premonition that everything would soon come to a head.

Steve's thoughts returned to Gary's so-called confession. He'd let Ed drown and never even told anyone he'd been with him. Steve wondered what he should do. After a while he decided the best thing would be to talk to Gran.

He ran up the stairs and knocked on her door.

'Come in,' said Mrs Fenton reluctantly. Steve opened the door, and forced himself to smile even though they disliked each other intensely. Years ago Steve had kicked a football through her front window and Mrs Fenton had demanded a huge price for the damage which he had had to pay out of his pocket money; he had been broke for months afterwards.

'Would you like a cup of tea downstairs, Mrs Fenton?' he asked, trying to curry favour. 'I'll sit with Gran.' He looked down at the bed and saw that Gran's eyes were closed. For a moment, he wondered if she was just pretending to sleep for he knew Gran disliked Mrs Fenton as much as he did.

'That *won't* be necessary. I was particularly asked not to leave your grandmother's side.'

'I want to talk to her.'

'She's asleep.'

'Are you sure?'

'She wouldn't have her eyes closed if she wasn't.' Mrs Fenton's big, broad pasty face ended in a rat-trap of a mouth and dozens of wobbling chins.

'I only want five minutes.'

'When she wakes.'

'That might not be for hours,' bellowed Steve, hoping he was getting through to Gran and that she would open her eyes and order Mrs Fenton from the room. But there wasn't even the slightest flicker.

'Listen, Steven,' Mrs Fenton hissed, 'you must try to understand that your grandmother is ill. She had a stroke, remember? She's really very poorly.'

'She was OK in hospital,' he protested.

'That's as maybe.' Mrs Fenton's tone was dismissive and Steve, feeling defeated, left the room.

Trying to keep control of his temper, Steve put his tea on a tray and went into the sitting room, switched on the TV and sat down on the sofa. Mum's sandwiches were good and so was the hot, strong tea, and in spite of Mrs Fenton, he soon felt better, particularly when he realised his favourite serial was on.

For a few glorious minutes, Steve managed to switch off from his anxieties about Gran's illness, the telephone calls and Gary's behaviour. In fact he was so exhausted and the food and TV were so comforting that he gradually drifted off to sleep on the sofa.

Ten minutes later, Steve jerked awake to the urgent and familiar ringing of the phone. Someone must have plugged the wretched thing in again and now the monster had woken. He was sure Mrs Fenton was responsible.

Steve sat on the sofa as if he was encased in concrete.

The ringing seemed to become increasingly

urgent, and as the tone sharpened, he felt as if his will was once again being broken. Feeling ice cold, despite the warmth of the room and the sunlight outside, Steve walked zombie-like to the phone and picked up the receiver, expecting to hear static. But, instead, there was a short silence.

'Why did you take so long to answer?' demanded Gary.

'I've been asleep.'

'I don't think I'm ever going to sleep again.'

'What's happened?'

'You've got to promise me you won't tell.' Gary's voice was threatening and fearful at the same time.

'I told you, I can't do that.'

'So what are you going to do then?'

'I don't know. I'm still thinking about it. Why don't you go to the police yourself and tell them what happened?'

'I can't.'

'Better get it over.' Steve wondered why he was being so insistent, for if Gary was telling the truth, his 'confession' wouldn't change anything.

'I'm not going anywhere.' His voice was

suddenly full of desperate menace. 'And if you grass me up, you'll never be safe.'

'What else happened?'

'I don't get you.'

'There's something else, isn't there?'

'I told you the truth.'

'I've got a hunch –'

'Yes?' began Gary aggressively. 'What kind of a hunch?'

'I don't think you're telling me the whole truth.'

'You don't?' Gary was more alarmed than threatening now.

'Go to the police,' repeated Steve. 'Tell *them* the whole truth. Get it over with. It's the only way.'

'I want to see you.'

'No way.'

'I want to see you now.'

Gary seemed so full of authority that Steve almost lost his nerve. 'What for?' he muttered.

'We need to talk some more.'

Steve felt a rush of anger. He was determined not to be terrorised and knew he had to stand up to Gary, but on the other hand if he did see him he might say more.

'All right.'

'What do you mean, all right?' Did Gary sound slightly thrown?

'I'll meet you behind the post office.' Steve knew there was a strip of wasteland behind the building. If they had to fight at least they wouldn't be anywhere near the river.

'OK.'

'I'm leaving now.' Steve slammed down the receiver and hurried to the door, determined not to let his new-found courage run out on him. Then he came to a juddering halt.

The phone was ringing again. He ran back and picked up the receiver, listening to the static with a new dread. But no voice broke through.

Hurriedly he put the receiver down. Just in case it did.

14

Gary's just rung – he wants to meet me – now I really am scared. I know I've got to go, I know it's the only way I'm going to learn the truth, but I'm very worried about what he might do.

Wish me luck...

Gary was already waiting at the back of the post office, standing in the centre of the wasteland, hands on hips, looking warily arrogant. Did he have a weapon, wondered Steve, feeling apprehensive, sure now that he had not only been pushed into a confrontation he was going to deeply regret, but also certain he had completely mishandled the situation. Maybe Gary was planning to kill him. After all, if he was out of the way, Gary would be safe. There could be no doubt about that, but the point was, was Gary capable of committing such a crime? Had he had some practice?

Feeling weak and light-headed Steve began to

advance on Gary who was waiting for him, a quiet, calm, confident smile playing on his lips. Never had he felt in such a hopeless position. Looking up he saw rain clouds were obliterating the sun yet again and the wasteland had a dark, gloomy feel.

When he got close, Steve came to a halt. 'What do you want then?'

'I'm going to beat the hell out of you.'

'You reckon so?'

'I think that'll convince you.'

'What about?'

'Not to grass me up.'

Steve clenched his fists and they slowly advanced on each other. But as he prepared to receive a hefty punch, a low ringing sound began. It was all on one note, continuous and threatening, but not like a telephone at all.

'What's that?' demanded Gary uneasily.

'Sounds like a burglar alarm. We'd better go and see,' Steve said, seizing the opportunity to postpone the fight.

'What's the point?' demanded Gary, but Steve was already sprinting back over the rough ground towards the little alley that ran along the side of the post office.

Steve felt the terror clutch at his insides as the ringing speeded up a little. Suddenly, however, his fears dropped away and he realised that he didn't have to be scared any more. The voice on the telephone could surely be none other than that of an old friend, reaching out to him from beyond the grave.

All four phone boxes in front of the post office were making the same continuous, low ringing sound. Steve gazed at them, conscious that Gary would be with him at any moment. He had never heard a telephone sound quite like this before. He had a feeling of anticipation, a surety that he was not going to be beaten up after all, that he was going to be saved.

The phones continued to ring, their pitch sharpening a little, and Steve hurried towards the nearest box, opened the door, picked up the phone and listened to the familiar static. When he put down the receiver, however, the ringing started all over again. Steve hesitated. Then he felt a presence and turned round to see Gary standing in the small square outside the post office, unmoving, as if he had been turned to stone. Not even a strand of his hair seemed to blow in the light wind, nor did his eyes appear to blink.

Suddenly, as if on some unspoken command, other phones began to ring inside the post office and the noise level rose to such a pitch that it was painful.

Soon the phones were shrilling from the betting shop, the bakery, the toy shop, the flats, the sorting office, a couple of parked cars and the florist's. Then the entire contents of a mobile phone shop began to shrill on the same high note, growing sharper every moment.

Dazed, Steve opened the door to step outside, and immediately wished he hadn't. Outside, the noise was so much more painful, as if the ringing was driving little metal spikes into his head.

Gary began to move, half turning towards the phone shop, and as he did so the ringing became a searing electronic scream. He put his hands over his ears and slowly sank to his knees. Steve also found the pain becoming increasingly unbearable, the sound spikes piercing the inside of his skull, making his brain feel as if it was going to explode. He couldn't think straight any more, only feel the electronic scream in his head, and the more he pressed his hands over his ears the louder and more penetrating the sound became.

Stop it, Ed. You've got to stop it!

The phones were densely packed on the shelves of the shop, some in boxes, some on display, and they were all making the same scream. Steve had never seen a collection of mobile phones look so evil before with their display screens like the gash of a leering mouth, their keypads as black as night, their cases pulsating.

Stop it, Ed! You've got to stop. Stop for me.

The phones continued to shrill and then came to a sudden halt. The unexpected silence was like the most refreshing, tranquil pool of calm. People were crowding into the previously empty square now, gazing at the silent phones in disbelief.

Gary staggered to his feet and stumbled over to Steve, all his malevolent aggression gone.

'Suppose they start again?'

'They won't,' replied Steve uncertainly. 'We're going to be all right.'

'He's doing this, isn't he? He kept calling you…and then he started on me. Like with the mobile on the bus.'

'Who are you talking about?' Steve needed him to continue. He didn't want to be reassuring for he was suddenly sure that Gary had more, far more, to tell him.

'He's doing it, isn't he? Ed's making the phones ring. I can't stand it any more.' Gary was sweating and there were little trails of saliva dribbling down his lips.

Steve seized the opportunity. 'You know how you can stop him. Just own up.'

'What to? To him climbing the tree and falling in the river and me not being able to save him?'

'Just tell the police exactly what happened.'

'I can't. I can't tell them that. I'll get banged up.'

Steve realised the moment of truth had come. 'You mean there is more than you've told me? Tell me before the phones start up again,' he demanded, instinctively using the phones as his own weapon against Gary.

Gary began to speak in a rush, as if the words were tumbling out of their own accord and he was no longer in control of what he was saying.

'Ed's adventures got a bit tame so I thought I'd liven them up.'

'How did you do that?' demanded Steve.

'We started these dares, one after the other, and neither of us would back down. Not ever.' Gary's voice was so low now that Steve could hardly hear him.

'So?'

'I dared Ed he wouldn't walk into Safeway and nick some beer. Just like I had.'

'You mean you'd –'

'The day before I stole four cans of lager. Ed had to get six.'

'And did he?'

'No.'

Steve breathed a sigh of heartfelt relief. 'What happened next?'

'We met up by the river.'

'And he told you he wasn't going through with the dare.'

'That's right.'

'What did you do?'

'I laughed at him. Called him chicken. He didn't like that.'

'He wouldn't,' said Steve grimly.

'So...I...he tried to smack me one.'

'Yes?'

'I pushed him and he went in. Like I said. It wasn't my fault. I didn't push him hard. He must have slipped as well and –'

Steve looked blankly at Gary. He didn't feel hatred. Just shock. The same kind of shock that Gary might have felt. And as for Ed…

'You'd better get down to the police station. Tell them what really happened.'

'They'll nick me.'

'Better than Ed contacting you on a thousand phones.'

They stared at each other suspiciously.

'I can't just give myself up.'

'Why not?' demanded Steve. As if on cue. As if on cue, the phones started to ring again. Their electronic scream was twice as penetrating and the crowd hurried out of the square.

Gary was on his knees, his hands over his ears, whimpering piteously. Steve felt like doing the same, but to ease the pain a little, he dived back into one of the phone boxes, slamming the door shut. Focusing on the phone that was ringing incessantly in front of him, he picked up the receiver and listened. Then a familiar voice just penetrated the static.

'Is that you, Stevie? Is that you?'

'It's me.' He spoke with conviction, knowing exactly what he should say, despite the fact that his heart was pumping so hard. 'It's all right now. Gary's going to confess. He's going to the police. Stop the ringing, Ed. You've got to stop the ringing now!'

The static increased and there was no trace of Ed's voice any more. Steve hung up, but immediately the phone started to ring again.

Outside, the electronic scream was as loud as ever and Gary was still on his knees.

Would Ed's campaign *ever* stop? Didn't he know now not to go to extremes? But Ed always went to extremes.

A police car drove slowly into the square and stopped. The officer got out, staring round him in surprise.

Then, just as suddenly as they had begun, the phones stopped ringing and the resulting silence was unearthly, like a soft reviving blanket. Gary slowly rose to his feet, gazing around him as if it was a trick and the electronic scream would start again at any moment. Then he saw the police officer and turned almost gratefully towards him.

Gary was talking urgently to the officer, rather as if he was a priest to whom he was making a welcome confession. As Steve approached, Gary broke off and said, 'I'm going down the nick.' His eyes were full of tears.

'Will you be long?' he asked.

'That depends,' interrupted the officer. 'He's going to need his parents and a solicitor.'

'Shall I call them?' asked Steve. He wanted to let Ed know that justice had been done at last.

'We'll do that,' said the police officer, leading Gary to one of the squad cars. As they drove away Steve could see Gary peering from the window as if he was taking his last glimpse of a free world, but a world that had become unbearable to him.

When Steve returned home, his parents were still out and the phone was ringing. He waited for a long time before picking up the receiver, gazing down at it, wondering if Ed was still dissatisfied.

'Hello?' Steve asked hesitantly.

'Mr Parker?' There was no static and the voice was weary but polite.

'I'm his son.'

'Is Mr Parker available?'

'He's out. Can I take a message.'

'It's the exchange. We wanted to apologise for the fault on your telephone which has now been rectified.'

'Are you sure?' asked Steve doubtfully.

'Quite sure.' The operator sounded slightly offended.

'I've just come back from Hunter Square. All the phones were ringing –'

'Yes,' the operator replied, obviously having been told many times before. 'The incident is being investigated. Now, as I'm sure you realise, we've got hundreds of other subscribers to call. Everything should be back to normal now.'

Everything? Steve put down the receiver, feeling that nothing would ever be normal again.

When he knocked tentatively on his grandmother's bedroom door, there was no reply so he walked straight in to find Mrs Fenton had nodded off to sleep in her chair and Gran was sitting bolt upright in bed, gazing at her beadily.

'Just take a look at that,' she snapped. 'The sentry's gone to sleep on her job. Doesn't she deserve a court-martial?'

'You bet,' said Steve with great pleasure.

'Oi, you!' Gran yelled, her illness apparently

forgotten. 'Wakey, wakey!'

Mrs Fenton opened her eyes and jerked upright. 'I'm so sorry. I was –'

'Asleep?' Gran was unpleasantly sarcastic. 'Go down to the kitchen and make me a cup of tea. I want to talk to my grandson. Alone.'

'But –' Mrs Fenton was on her feet in a terrible fluster.

'Don't "but" me,' commanded Gran. 'And make the tea strong.'

Mrs Fenton staggered from the room, closing the door behind her.

'I hear you've been having trouble with the phone,' said Gran.

'It's over now. The exchange fixed the fault.' Could he confide in her, wondered Steve. Then he decided to go ahead and do just that. 'There was all this static when I picked up the receiver. But I thought I heard Ed's voice and then I thought I heard him on lots of other phones. I expect you think I've been hearing things.'

'What did he say?'

'Mostly, "Are you there, Stevie? Are you there?" And, once, "I got drowned, didn't I?" He decided against telling her that Ed had tried to contact Gary too.

'Do you know what really happened that day by the river?'

'I do now.'

'Was someone with Ed?'

'Yes.'

'What's this person doing now?'

'He's talking to the police.'

'Voluntarily?'

'Yes.'

'Was it an accident?'

'Sort of.'

'Are you going to tell your parents?'

'About the drowning? Yes.'

'But not the voices?'

'They'd think I'd gone mad.'

There was a short silence.

'Do you think I'm mad too?' asked Steve anxiously.

'No.' Gran was gazing up at him, calmly and steadily.

'Then what *do* you think?'

'From what you've said, Ed had a lot of will power.'

Steve nodded.

'Funny how strong the will can be,' said Gran, lying back on her pillows and smiling up at Steve.

'You've got a lot of that too, Gran.'

She winked at him. 'Takes one to know one,' she replied quietly. 'Now, where's that tea?'

That night, Steve went up to his room, sat on his bed and read through all the 'Fors' and 'Againsts' he had written in his diary. He had a hollow feeling inside.

Then he began to write slowly and painfully:

It's all over – Gary has confessed and I should feel happy but I don't. I feel sad and lonely. As I came up the stairs I was willing the phone to ring but nothing happened. I so want to talk to Ed. More than anything in the world I want to hear his voice again. But I know I won't. If I ever did...

Downstairs the phone began to ring again.